Thanks to the dive guide and
the owner of the no-name café in Cambridge
for sharing their life stories with me.
Thanks to the people I met.

— T. L.

HERE & There

THEA LU

EERDMANS BOOKS FOR YOUNG READERS

GRAND RAPIDS, MICHIGAN

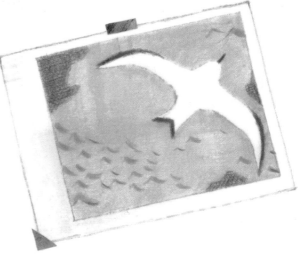

Here

There

This is Dan.

He is the owner
of a café,
living in a small town
by the sea.

This is Aki.

He is a sailor on
the sea, traveling from
place to place.

Dan lives a life
like a big oak tree,
rooted in his town
and never moving.

He always says:
"Just come.
I'm right here."

Aki lives a life
like a nomadic gull,
always on the wing
and never settling down.

He always says:
"Hey, I'm going
there!"

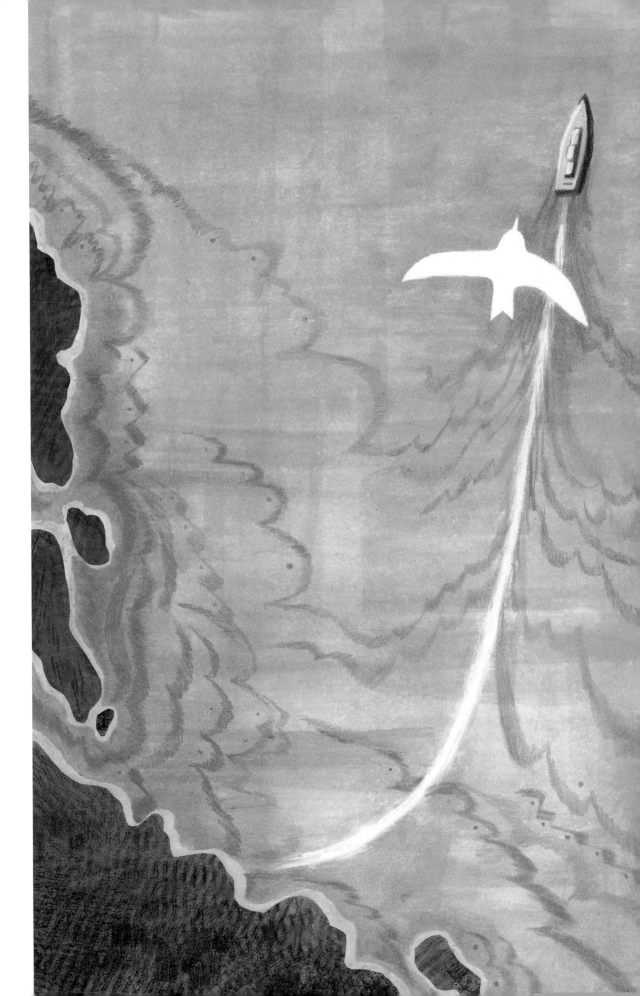

Dan likes his life—
it gives him a strong
sense of belonging.

Aki also likes his life—
it never lacks colorful wonders
along the way.

Outside Dan's window is the view
he has known for his whole life.

He's never seen places far away from
his town.

When the wind is blowing, he sometimes
wonders what life is like in other places.

Next to Aki's window
is the engine room where his bed is for now.

He's never had a place to call home.

When the machine is booming, he sometimes
wishes for an old friend to talk with.

In moments like those,

they feel so distanced from the world.

A morning at the café
usually starts like this:

When everything is ready,
Dan opens the door,
looking forward to
the people who stop in.

A journey at sea
usually goes like this:

When he arrives in a port,
Aki drops the anchor,
thinking about the people
he might meet.

Once a couple visited from the far east.
They talked all about the treasures
in their ancient city.

Once a man visited from the far north.
He told Dan stories about his life
in his snowy country.

Once at a fishing town, a fisherman
invited Aki to stay overnight.
The bedding was soft and the room was warm.

Once in a harbor village, a family shared
their food with Aki. Children gathered
to hear his stories about the sea.

And once a lady visited from
the far south. She described
to Dan the magical landscapes
around her homeland.

And once on an island,
the locals let Aki join their
gathering on the sand. Songs
flew around a dancing bonfire.

Dan has a wall filled with keepsakes
people have given him. Looking at them,
he feels like the frames are little
windows, each opening a piece of
the world to him—such as this one.

Aki has a notebook where he puts photos of people he's met. Looking at them, he feels like the photos are little houses, each bringing a sense of home for him—such as this one.

In moments like these,

On that day, there were people from all different lands and among them, there was a man from the sea.

Stories from all kinds of places filled the room.

On that day, lovely people
gathered together in a café, and
the owner felt like an old friend.

Laughter, as if they were a family,
echoed under the roof.

they both feel
so close to the world.

THEA LU is an illustrator, designer, and picture book maker based in Shanghai. She earned an MA in design strategy from China's Tsinghua University and an MA in children's book illustration from the Cambridge School of Art. Thea's work has won the Sebastian Walker Award in the UK and has also been honored in Italy, Poland, and China. *Here and There* is her picture book debut. Visit Thea's website at thealu.net or follow her on Instagram @lu_thea.

Text and illustrations © 2022 Thea Lu
Translation rights arranged through the VeroK Agency, Barcelona, Spain

Originally written in Chinese and English by Thea Lu
English-language translation © 2024 Thea Lu

First published in the United States in 2024
by Eerdmans Books for Young Readers,
an imprint of Wm. B. Eerdmans Publishing Co.
Grand Rapids, Michigan

www.eerdmans.com/youngreaders

Manufactured in China

33 32 31 30 29 28 27 26 25 24   1 2 3 4 5 6 7 8 9 10

ISBN 978-0-8028-5623-4

A catalog record of this book is available from the Library of Congress.

MIX
Paper | Supporting responsible forestry
FSC
www.fsc.org   FSC® C104723